Princess of the Sea

Neda Fatima

Ukiyoto Publishing

All global publishing rights are held by
Ukiyoto Publishing
Published in 2024

Content Copyright © Neda Fatima
ISBN 9789362695888

All rights reserved.
No part of this publication may be reproduced, transmitted, or stored in a retrieval system, in any form by any means, electronic, mechanical, photocopying, recording or otherwise, without the prior permission of the publisher.
The moral rights of the author have been asserted.

This is a work of fiction. Names, characters, businesses, places, events, locales, and incidents are either the products of the author's imagination or used in a fictitious manner. Any resemblance to actual persons, living or dead, or actual events is purely coincidental.

This book is sold subject to the condition that it shall not by way of trade or otherwise, be lent, resold, hired out or otherwise circulated, without the publisher's prior consent, in any form of binding or cover other than that in which it is published.

www.ukiyoto.com

This book is dedicated to my daughter Aayat Fatima, my mother Shahina Siddiqui, my father Late Rais Ahmad siddiqui and my whole family.

Do you know that the clear water of the blue sea that is surging and swirling is very deep. Very deep. Reaching its bottom is not a child's play. Reaching there is a big thing, you people cannot even imagine what is there inside the water.

Perhaps you will say that what is there to think about its bottom? At the most there will be only sandy land there. But no. It is not so. You will be surprised to know that God's nature has inhabited a world there too. There are very strange trees and flowers there which you would have never seen on this earth. Those trees and flowers are very beautiful and flexible. They get startled even by the slightest movement of the waves of the sea as if they are some living thing. And you will be even more surprised to know that thousands of small and big fishes of different colours and varieties live on these trees just like different kinds of birds live on our land trees. And much below the sand, there is a luxurious royal palace. This palace is decorated with colourful seashells and big precious pearls. The king of fishes Sumarat lives in this palace.

It is mentioned once that many 100 years ago, the king of fishes Sumarat lived in that palace.

He had six innocent little girls. But after a few days Sumarat's queen Aajra died. Sumarat was very saddened by Aajra's death because he loved her very much. That is why Sumarat did not marry again after Aajra's death and Sumarat's old mother Rizala Bibi had to take care of the upbringing of his six little girls Sona, Heeri, Ana, Lima, Reeka, Turin.

Sumarat's old mother Rizala Bibi was a very intelligent woman. But she was very proud of the fact that she was the mother of king Sumarat. Because of her royal blood, she never used to talk directly to other common fishes.

But Rizala Bibi loved her granddaughters very much. She always used to treat them with love. And she often told them stories about the land world above the ocean.

Although all the six granddaughters of Rizala Bibi were very beautiful, the youngest princess Turin was extremely beautiful. Her complexion was white and spotless and her eyes were deep and blue like the sea. All the princesses used to listen to Rizala Bibi about the situation above the sea with great interest. But the youngest princess Turin used to get lost in listening to the situation there. And used to reach that world in her thoughts. Turin had told her grandmother Rizala Bibi many times about her desire to travel the world, but Rizala Bibi would give her the same answer every time -

"No Turin, you are still very young. When you turn 15 years old, then you will be able to go there".

Like this, time passed and the desire to see the world above kept increasing in Turin's heart. Finally a day came when Rizala Bibi told all the sisters that the eldest princess Sona has turned 15 years old. So if she wants, she can travel above the sea.

Each princess was 1 year younger than the other. According to this, Turin still needed 5 more years to see that world. Still Sona promised that whatever she sees there, she will tell everyone everything. So one day Rizala Bibi gave permission to Sona princess to go above after dressing her up properly and explaining some important things to her. All the other princesses watched her go with longing eyes and started waiting impatiently for the time when she will come down and tell them about the place.

When Sona princess returned to her palace from the surface of the sea, she was overjoyed. Everyone quickly took her to the garden of the palace and there, sitting in the colourful fragrant sea bushes, Sona princess started telling in a very nice way with a smile on her face.

"Oh, I am stunned. I am telling you the truth, I was totally stunned. After going to the upper world, I came to know that we are actually living in a prison. This palace of ours is a prison cell of blue water.

All the sisters were listening to her every word with great attention but Princess Turin was lost in the words of Princess Sona. When Princess Sona stopped speaking for a little while, she became restless and said-

"Yes sister! Tell me quickly. Then what did you see there?" Princess Sona said-

"Sitting on a small sandy rock there, I saw that big ships were floating on the surface of the sea. And there was dry land on the shore of the sea. There was a very big city on that land. There were countless houses in the city. People were living in those houses. These houses were glittering with different kinds of lights. Bells were ringing repeatedly in the city. Very melodious and sweet songs were echoing in those houses. The sounds of those bells and songs are still delightful in my ears. There was a lot of hustle and bustle in the city. I really wanted to reach the shore and see the city more closely but I regretted not doing so because Grandma had already denied permission. I had the sky above my head and when I reached the surface, it was night and the moon was shining in the sky. Around which there was a network of small stars. And when I started returning from there, the night had passed and instead of the moon and stars, the sun was spreading light everywhere with its golden rays. This light was looking very good to my eyes and I did not want to leave from there but what could I do, Grandma did not allow me to stay for long".

All these scenes started dancing like a picture in front of the eyes of Turin princess. If she had her way, she would have rushed to that rock and come out of that prison of blue water and would have seen all those things in the light of the sun and moon to her heart's content that her elder sister princess Sona had mentioned. But she could not do that now because according to her grandmother, she was only 10 years old.

In the second year, the second princess, Heeri princess, also became capable of going to the surface of the sea. When she reached there, it was evening time and the sun was setting in the sky. The sight of the setting sun seemed very beautiful to her eyes. The sky was looking like a very big plate of gold. Its reflection was falling on the sea as well, and the colour of the sea had also turned red. And the clouds in the sky were looking like white cotton, but as soon as the sun hid, darkness covered all that redness. That night, since the sky was overcast, the Heeri princess could not see the moon and stars despite waiting for a long time. Finally, at midnight, she got tired of the darkness and went back to her palace.

The next year, the third sister Princess Ana came up. She was the most mischievous and daring of all her sisters. That is why when she reached the surface of the sea, she swam into the river that fell into the sea. When she looked up from the white water of the river and saw blue valleys, black mountains and green grass on both the banks, she was very happy. Small birds were singing sweet songs in the grass. She liked these songs very much, so she memorized the lyrics of some of them. She was humming those songs in her heart. Suddenly the sun came out and the princess started feeling her body burning due to the bright rays of the sun. She took a long dip to cool herself and after some time came back to the surface of the river and saw small human children near her. These children were very beautiful. And the princess was very surprised to see that unlike fish, none of those children had a tail. But everyone was swimming like fish in the river. Princess Ana wanted to play with them but as soon as she reached near them, she saw a black, big and scary animal. Actually, it was the dog of those children and Princess Ana had never seen a dog before that. The dog started barking so loudly on seeing Princess Ana's face that the poor girl, with the desire to play with those children in her heart, again jumped into the depths of the ocean. And from there, when she dived, she took a breath only after reaching her palace.

The fourth princess, Lima, was very timid. And when she turned 15 and came to the surface of the sea, she stayed in the middle of the sea. Actually, she had heard very scary things about fishermen from her old grandmother Rizala Bibi. She was afraid to go to the shore lest some fisherman had spread his net there to catch fish. As long as Princess Lima remained on the surface, she kept looking at the ships with a pounding heart. She did not like the rumbling of the ships too much. So, before the sun set, she got bored and went back to her palace.

A year later, it was the turn of the fifth princess, Princess Reeka. Reeka was born in the winter season. All the other sisters came to the surface of the sea in the summer season. Only Reeka came in the winter season. That is why what she saw in that season, no other sister of hers had been able to see till now.

When she reached the surface of the sea, heavy gusts of cold wind were playing with the waves of the sea and she started feeling as if she was swinging in a swing and not in the water of the sea. Apart from that, heavy pieces of white ice were floating here and there on the surface of the sea. Many of those pieces were bigger than human houses. And all those pieces were shining like diamonds in the sunlight. She sat down on a piece of ice with great pride and started enjoying herself by spreading herself on its soft surface. Suddenly the sky was covered with clouds in the evening. She was a bit surprised to hear the thunder of the clouds at first but then she started liking it. Rather, she started spreading herself and imitating that thunder. Meanwhile, heavy rain started. She kept playing with the raindrops for a long time. She kept dancing and singing here and there in the flash of lightening. And finally, when she became tired and exhausted, and started feeling the need to rest, she went back to her palace. Except for the youngest princess, Princess Turin, all the other sisters had grown up and were now given complete freedom by their old grandmother Rizala Bibi to go to the sea surface. Whenever they felt bored in their palace, they used to come to the sea surface to get some fresh air and would keep themselves entertained by the views outside for a long time. All the sisters had very melodious voices. They got great pleasure by singing together on the sea surface. And the youngest princess, Turin, used to sit in a corner of the shiny palace and wait for the day when she would also be able to go up like her sisters.

Finally, the youngest princess's wait ended and one day early in the morning, her old grandmother Rizala Bibi smilingly told her -

"Congratulations, my child. Today you have turned 15 years old". And after that, Rizala Bibi lovingly kissed her spotless and rose petal-like soft skin and said -

"May God protect you from evil eyes. Though my daughter's beauty does not need any praise, still I will dress you in expensive clothes like your other sisters. So that you can travel the world above with your royal splendour".

And after saying this, the old grandmother stitched a beautiful white flower in her feathers and decorated her tail with 8-8 small but very colourful and precious stones and it was as if the moon and stars of the sky started shining in Turin's eyes. Her heart was dancing with joy. After so much waiting, now she was going to the island of her dreams.

When the princess reached the surface of the sea and raised her head, the sun was setting at that time. But the colour of the clouds was still red. As if someone had sprinkled gulal on the sky. And on the surface of the sea, a ship was moving as if a bird was flying in the sky in joy. As soon as the pink clouds of the evening sank into the deep darkness, thousands of types of lights lit up in that ship and the dark night suddenly became a city of lights and the people sitting in the ship started singing very melodious songs.

The princess was so engrossed in listening to those songs that suddenly a strong storm wave threw her very close to the ship and when she emerged from the surface of the sea, she also saw the people sitting in the ship. Among all of them was sitting a prince named Fahad. Fahad was the most handsome of all of them. His big eyes were as black as the night. He was definitely not more than 16 years old. Today was his birthday. That is why all the people sitting in the ship were dancing and singing. After singing, those people started dancing on the rope of the ship and along with their steps, it seemed as if the princess's heart also started dancing. And she started singing her sea song in slow tunes. Suddenly there was a strong tide in the sea which shook such a big ship. For a moment, the princess also dived into the water in fear. And after the second moment when she came out, all the lanterns of the ship had been extinguished and there was pitch darkness all around. In that pitch darkness, when the lightening flashed in the sky and gave some light, Turin saw that the ship had broken into pieces after hitting the stormy waves and Prince Fahad was floating in the water.

Turin had heard from her grandmother that when a person drowns in water, his life ends. Her whole body started trembling at the thought of the prince's life ending. And she saw that Prince Fahad had become completely exhausted while swimming. His arms and legs were tired and worn out. His big black eyes were closing. When the princess saw his condition, she reached him with all her might, hitting the waves. And pulling him by his long hair, she took him to the shore and threw him on the cold sand there. Prince Fahad had fainted due to exhaustion. Turin sat beside him in the sand all night. She kept kissing his feet again and again, kept looking at his face, his eyes and his hair with happiness and surprise and when the morning came and the bells started ringing in the city and light started spreading everywhere, the princess quickly hid herself in the foam on the shore so that no one could see her. And she started waiting for someone else to come to help Prince Fahad. The princess did not have to wait for long. When a fisherman from the royal palace passing by the shore saw the prince, he was very surprised to see Prince Fahad in this condition and started shouting loudly. Hearing the noise of the fisherman, many people gathered there and during this time Prince Fahad's body also started moving. Fahad started smiling seeing so many people around him and he thanked all those people. He had no idea that Turin had saved his life. And when Fahad went from there to his palace with other men, Turin also became sad and jumped into the sea and came to her palace.

When her five sisters, Sona, Heeri, Ana, Lima and Reeka asked her about the state of the world above, she could not tell them anything. Her heart was so sad that she did not feel like talking to anyone.

For many days, Princess Turin kept coming to the place where she had left Prince Fahad. But after that she could not see Fahad there and every time she would reach her palace more sad than before. Finally, she could not hide her sorrow for long and she told all her sisters about her meeting with that Prince Fahad. And she also told them that she wants to see that Prince Fahad again at any cost.

"What is the big deal in this?" Princess Sona replied after listening to her problem.

"I know very well where Prince Fahad's palace is. I can take you right now to that place on the seashore from where his palace is clearly visible."

When princess Turin heard this, she felt as if she had come back to life. Her heart started dancing with joy again. She said happily-

"My good sister Sona, show me that place right now".

And Princess Sona took him by the hand and took him to a place which was very close to Prince Fahad's palace. It was a beautiful palace made of pink stones. Inside it were small flower beds with colourful flowers. In the middle of those flower beds was a marble water tank. There were stone statues placed around the tank. Fountains were running around and very expensive silk curtains were waving in that palace. There were beautiful carvings on the walls and everywhere in the palace silver and gold chandeliers were glittering. Seeing the palace, Princess Turin started rubbing her eyes as if she was seeing a golden dream.

Now that Turin had seen Prince Fahad's palace with her sister Sona, she would go there alone several times a day and would keep looking at that palace for hours. She would swim and reach the sand right on the shore and from there she could see the people walking and moving in the palace very clearly.

As she looked at the things in the palace and observed the lives of the people living there, she started liking human life more and more, and a desire to live such a life started to arise in her heart. When she saw that humans could travel on the surface of the sea in ships and fly among the clouds on the peaks of mountains, she would say with a sigh –

"I wish I was born as the daughter of a poor man instead of being born in the house of the king of the sea."

Various questions started to arise in her mind about the interesting and colourful life of humans. She had heard a lot about humans, yet she wanted to ask a lot more. But she understood very well that her sisters were not capable of answering all her questions. Finally, one day she asked her grandmother Rizala Bibi –

"Grandma, if men do not drown in water, do they remain alive forever? Do they not die like us?"

"Why don't they die?" Rizala Bibi said laughing at her granddaughter's innocence –

"They also die like us. Yes, but their life is much shorter than ours. We can live for 300 years, but I have heard that when humans die, their souls do not die."

"And when we die?" the princess asked in surprise.

"After death, our bodies turn into foam, and our souls also die. Once we die, we do not get a new life."

"Oh, so grandmother, it is better to get a human soul than to live for 300 years. Oh, how fun human life is."

And grandmother said staring at the innocent Turin –

"You should not think such things. How can human life be compared to our life! We live a life of comfort and peace many times more than them." And on hearing this from Rizala Bibi, Princess Turin muttered to herself, "What kind of a life is this? One day I will become the foam on the seashore and will neither be able to listen to the songs of the waves nor play with the colourful flowers. The moon, stars and the waving pieces of clouds of the upper world will disappear from my sight forever".

And then, after thinking for some time, Turin's eyes started shining and she said, "Grandma, is there any way by which I too can get a soul that will never die?" And Rizala Bibi looked at her with great disinterest and said, "No, this cannot happen". And then, after thinking for a while, she said, "Many years ago, I had asked the sea-dwellers the same question and they had told me that we can get the souls of humans in only one way". "What is that?" Turin asked impatiently. "When a person loves us so much that he doesn't even love his parents. But this is not possible. Why did humans start loving us so much? Every fish in our world considers its tail to be its most precious jewel and humans laugh at this. They prefer two legs more than the tail. They find their legs more beautiful than the tail and then I have also heard from the midwives that they consider us their delicious food".

On hearing this, Turin looked at her tail and heaved a sigh and started thinking about something. While thinking, sometimes the images of the midwives of the sea and sometimes the prince of the land started moving in front of her eyes. While thinking, suddenly she thought of something that changed all her sadness into a smile and the winding paths of the midwives' hut started spreading in front of her eyes. At night, when Rizala Bibi and her father Sumarat and all her sisters fell asleep, Turin quietly left her palace and headed towards the hut of the midwives of the sea. She was sure that when the midwives of the sea would listen to her heart, their hearts would melt and they would definitely help her. After all, the midwives cannot be so harsh as to rebuke her outright.

The way to the midwives' hut was very dangerous. The path from the bottom of the sea to their hut had thick bushes of sharp and poisonous thorns. But Turin somehow managed to reach there, avoiding those bushes. There was no fruit or flower anywhere near the midwives' hut. Everywhere there were bones of those people who drowned in the sea. These bones were the food of the midwives and around the midwives there was a web of big, dangerous snakes.

The midwives laughed loudly as soon as they saw her, "I know why you have come to me. Foolish princess!" And the snakes around started moving loudly.

When Turin heard this, her heart sank. She became so sad that tears started appearing in her eyes.

"Hey crazy girl! Why are you crying? What I mean to say is that whatever you have thought is not right. You will ruin yourself like this. You still have days of fun and frolic. You still have many years to live. But what disease have you contracted on your life? You want to get rid of your tail forever and get a human form. So that the prince also starts loving you and you win his love and get a soul that will never die. Isn't that what you want?" After saying this, the midwives again started laughing like mad and poor Turin kept crying in the same sad way.

"Well, if you insist, I will fulfil this wish of yours. Now you are happy, right?"

And Turin's weeping eyes actually started laughing and the midwife said very seriously -

"I will give you a medicine. Take that medicine with you and immediately reach the seashore and drink it before the sun rises. As soon as you drink it, your tail will disappear and you will also get a human-like appearance and you will also be able to walk on two legs like humans. But remember one thing that you will feel pain while walking, you will feel as if sharp needles are pricking your feet. But despite this, whoever sees you will not be able to stop praising your beauty. Even in dancing, no great dancer will be able to compete with you. But you will definitely feel pain while dancing. If you are ready to bear this pain, then I will give you that medicine".

"I will bear everything" – the princess replied in a trembling voice – "Give me the medicine"

"There is still time. Think once again". The midwives started speaking in a thundering voice –

"If you change your human form once, then you will never be able to get your present form again. Then you will never be able to walk inside the sea like this. You will have to leave your sisters, your beloved father and your old grandmother forever. And also remember that if you are unable to win the love of that prince and the prince is unable to love you more than his parents and if he is unable to marry you, then you will never get a soul that will never die, and the next day after he gets married, you will turn into foam on the seashore as soon as the sun rises".

Turin's face turned pale, but still she kept up her courage and said - "I have thought of everything. Give me that medicine". And the princess asked in surprise - "Price? What will be the price?"

"You don't know that there is a great magic in your voice. I myself like this voice of yours very much. You will have to give your melodious voice in exchange for my medicine. You probably don't know that the medicine I am going to give you is very expensive. I will have to mix my blood in this medicine".

"But" Turin said in a frightened voice - "If you take my voice from me, then what will I be left with?"

"You will be left with your beautiful body, captivating eyes, long golden hair, your charming and unique style of dancing" and after saying this, the midwives once again became serious and said.

"But I am not forcing you to do this. Now think again for the last time, if you agree to this deal then come forward so that I can cut your tongue and give you that medicine".

After thinking for a while, Turin moved forward silently and Dai Maa cut her tongue in one stroke. And then she pricked her body with some sharp object and black blood started flowing from her body. Dai Maa put her blood in a vessel made of bones and put her saliva in that blood and after reciting some mantras, she blew on it and after that gave that vessel to Turin. It was as if Turin had got the kingdom of both the worlds. She happily flapped her feet and reached the sand on the seashore at a great speed. At that time, the grains of sand were shining like real pearls in the light of the moon and the palace of Prince Fahad in front was looking even more beautiful in that light. As soon as Turin reached the sand, she poured the medicine in her mouth and as soon as she drank it, she felt as if she had swallowed a lot of burning embers instead of medicine. Her body caught fire and she suddenly felt so much pain that she fainted, and when she regained consciousness, the bright rays of the sun were playing with the waves of the sea and Prince Fahad was standing in front of her. He was looking at her with a mixed feeling of surprise and happiness with his big black eyes. During that time, when Turin saw her face in the sea water, she came to know that her face had completely changed, she had become a beautiful human woman instead of a princess of fishes. Fahad asked very lovingly -

"Who are you? And why have you come here? In response to this question of Fahad, she fixed her eyes on the prince's face. Because she could not speak anything with her mouth, her midwife had cut her tongue. After that Prince Fahad took her to his palace and there she was dressed in very expensive clothes. In those clothes, not only of the palace but she was looking like the most beautiful woman of the whole world . But due to being dumb, she was not able to speak or sing. When the other girls of the palace came to the prince, they started singing in their melodious voices. Prince Fahad started dancing to their voices and Princess Turin started thinking in her heart that if she had a tongue today, she would have surely sung in the most melodious voice. After that, those girls started dancing. Seeing them dancing, Turin also got up from her place and started dancing the dance of sea fishes.

Everyone was stunned to see the dance of Princess Turin, no one had seen such a dance before, but while dancing, Princess Turin kept feeling sharp needles pricking the soles of her feet.

But she kept dancing without caring about her pain. Fahad also became happy to see Turin dancing and he declared that now in his life he will never let her separate from him. Turin started living happily in Fahad's palace. But at night, when everyone in the palace was fast asleep, Turin would come to the sparkling seashore and sit on the shore and dip her burning feet into the cool, clear water. This gave her great relief, and as she sat there, all kinds of thoughts about her real palace and her relatives would start to swim and flutter like fish in the sea in her mind.

One night, when she was sitting there, weaving the web of those thoughts, she heard some noise in the waves of the sea and when she raised her head, she saw all her five sisters there, holding each other in their arms. On seeing them, Turin's eyes started shining like stars with joy. All the five sisters also recognized Turin at first sight. They told her in their own language that they were very shocked by her separation. Her father, the king of fishes, Sumarat also misses her a lot and poor Rizala Bibi remains drowned in the sea of sorrow and grief for hours without her. They all requested her to come back to her old palace. Princess Turin understood everything they said but was not capable of answering anything. Still, her beautiful eyes were clearly saying that-

"O my dear sisters! How can I go into the sea now? Now, as soon as I go into the sea, I will drown like other people and as soon as I drown, my life will end and my bones will become food for the midwives of the sea".

After that day, her sisters started coming there every night to meet her. They used to bring roses from their royal garden for her every night. They used to entertain her by dancing in the waves of the sea and singing songs of their country. One night, Turin saw that along with her five sisters, her king father and old grandmother had also come to the surface of the sea after many years to see her. As soon as Rizala Bibi recognized her and spread her arms on the surface of the sea, Turin's heart was filled with emotion for a few moments on seeing the love of her poor grandmother, but now how could she go to her beloved grandmother. Turin told them through her eyes that she was very happy here and was living a very enjoyable life.

Indeed, Turin loved this place with all her heart. Though she still had love for her sisters, her father and her grandmother, she loved Prince Fahad the most and as days passed, Turin's love for Fahad was growing stronger. Being dumb, she could not speak anything but whenever she saw Fahad, the same question would flutter in her eyes -

"Don't you love me the most in this world?"

And it was as if Fahad understood the language of her eyes. Whenever his eyes met Turin's, he would say to her lovingly - "I love you very much. I cannot express my love in words". There was no doubt that Prince Fahad also loved her from the heart but the thought of making Turin his queen had never crossed his mind and until Princess Turin became Prince Fahad's queen, he could not get a soul that would never die. Still, Turin was sure that she would soon win over Fahad's heart and mind and Fahad would not like anyone else to be his queen except her. After all, where could he find a more beautiful wife than her. Days started passing like this. One day, King Abram of the neighbouring country Chhindwara sent a message of marriage for his daughter Sufia. Prince Fahad announced that he wanted to see the king's daughter Sufia princess on the pretext of a trip. That is why during dinner, Fahad asked Turin - "Are you not afraid of the sea? Would you like to travel with me in a ship?"

The journey of both of them started in the sea water. Turin's heart started beating with joy. What could be more joyful for her than this? Sitting in the ship, Fahad started telling Turin many things about the sea. Fahad liked the views of the sea very much. He was repeatedly praising the sea waves, birds and the beautiful fishes and Turin kept laughing in her heart after listening to his words. Because she knew much more about the world of the sea than him.

When Fahad fell asleep at night, Turin came on the top of the ship. It was not long since Turin had come to the dock of the ship that she saw her sisters. Her five sisters came very close to the dock of the ship while swimming and the princess started looking at Turin with very sad eyes. Because she understood that Turin had ended her freedom by changing the appearance of a human being. But Turin told them with the gestures of her eyes that she considered herself very lucky, the happiness and relief she was getting in that human world, cannot be found in the world of fishes even till the doomsday. At that time, a servant of the ship came out on the deck for some work and Turin's sisters immediately dived and disappeared and then Turin also went to her room.

Early next morning, the ship reached the port where Prince Fahad had to go. Countless soldiers and soldiers were standing on the shore to welcome Prince Fahad, dressed in their royal uniforms. Wherever Prince Fahad went, flowers were showered on him. The entire city was decorated like a bride. Turin was very happy to see that hustle and bustle, but Turin's happiness did not last long. At night, when King Abram of that country Chhindwara invited Prince Fahad, his companions and Turin for dinner, colourful candles were burning at many places there. The light of those candles made the night look like day, but there was more light on one face than those candles, in front of which all the candles looked dim and this face was of the King's own daughter Sufia. Fahad could not even imagine such a beautiful girl in his dreams. Fahad liked her very much and agreed to marry her. For Turin, it was as if all the candles had been extinguished and darkness began to descend before her eyes. In that darkness, she began to see the horrifying picture of her death again and again. Because she knew very well that if Prince Fahad married anyone else other than her, her silver-like shining white body would turn into foam. The next day Prince Fahad got married to Princess Sufia and in the evening he went to his tent with his wife. There was a great celebration in all the tents at night. When the girls started dancing after the song, Fahad signalled Turin to dance too. Although Turin's heart was sinking with the fear of her death, still she started dancing with great joy for the sake of her beloved prince . Turin's dance seemed to cast a spell on the hearts of the onlookers. While dancing, Turin again began to feel sharp needles pricking her feet, but this pain was not more than the pain she was feeling at the thought of being separated from that happy world forever. She was thinking that this night was the last night of her life and after that she would never be able to see her beloved prince Fahad for whom she had sacrificed her grandmother, her father, her sisters and even her tongue and left her entire world; she would be separated from him forever. "Ah! If only she had a tongue, she would have told Fahad that today he is celebrating his wedding on her dead body," thought Turin.

When these colourful parties ended, Fahad went to his tent with his new bride.

Turin, completely disheartened with her life, came and sat on the seashore. Sitting on the cold sand of the shore, she put her burning feet in the sea water and started looking at everything with astonished eyes. She started thinking that 'If it was in my control, I would never let the morning come.' Because she knew that the first ray of the sun would turn her body into foam. The words of the sea maids were echoing again and again in her beating heart - "Foolish princess! You will ruin yourself. You will have to leave your home and relatives for life, if the prince cannot marry you, you will turn into foam on the seashore." Suddenly Turin saw that her five sisters were swimming near her on the sea surface. But Turin was surprised to see that all of them had new long, colourful and beautiful feathers. Sensing Turin's surprise, Princess Sona told her -

" We have all handed over our old original feathers to the midwives of the sea"

" But why?" This question started troubling Turin's mind, but being dumb, she could not say anything and started staring at them. "We have given our feathers to the midwives to save your life," Princess Sona told her. "In exchange for our feathers, the midwives have given us this knife," and she showed Turin a sharp knife. "Before the sun rises, thrust that knife into Prince Fahad's heart." And as soon as Princess Sona heard this, Turin's heart skipped a beat, as if by saying this, her sister had thrust that sharp knife into her own heart. But Princess Sona continued to speak with the same impatience – "Look, now there is no time to think too much. There is very little time left for morning. Before the sun rises, thrust that knife into Prince Fahad's heart and drink his hot blood at the same time. The midwives have told us that as soon as you drink the prince's hot blood, you will again get the shape of a fish like before and then like us, you will also be able to live for 300 years. Grandma has obtained this knife after a lot of persuasion with the midwives. We will wait for you tomorrow morning". And after saying this, princess Sona threw that sharp knife on the sand at the shore and then she went back.

After she left, Turin picked up that sharp knife and remained lost in thoughts for some time and then without knowing what she was thinking, she quietly went to Prince Fahad's tent. Prince Fahad was fast asleep. The new bride was also sleeping beside him. Turin came close to Fahad and saw that Prince Fahad's face was looking even more charming in sleep. Turin looked at Fahad with loving eyes, then looked at that sharp knife and then looked at the bride. Her heart ached at the thought of ruining the life of the new bride by taking Fahad's life and her long thick eyelashes got wet with tears and she ran like a mad woman and again came to the sea shore and as soon as she reached there, she threw that sharp knife in the waves of the sea and herself lay down on the cold sand.

When the first ray of the sun spread, Turin's playful and butter-like soft body melted and turned into white foam. Gradually the rays of the sun began to fall on the foam, and Turin felt as if it were evaporating. "Where am I?" Turin started hovering in the air as a question.

"Dear princess. You are among the fairies of the air." She heard this voice in a very slow but very sweet tone-

"Your true love and sacrifice made you immortal." And in this way Turin, the princess of the sea, became a cool breeze of soft and fragrant air and many times in pleasant weather you must have felt that a cool breeze passes by playing with your hair. This cool breeze is actually the same sea princess Turin, who loves innocent children and flowers very much, who now, taking the form of air, always fills the hearts of humans with the colours of happiness and freshness.

About the Author

Neda Fatima

Neda Fatimais an Assistant professor by profession and lives in Lucknow, India. She has a passion for writing stories and poems. Earlier. she has written a book Attu ki kahaniyan Attu ki zubani in Hindi which was a children fiction book. Her 2 other books published are anthologies named S p milleur monophony and Rue.

www.ingramcontent.com/pod-product-compliance
Lightning Source LLC
LaVergne TN
LVHW041603070526
838199LV00047B/2125